I had to admit that I was feeling pretty flattered about being chosen for Miss Keller's writing class . . . but there were all those rumors about her. Like, she had an evil temper, held grudges, and took a deep and abiding personal dislike to some of her students, and that in her entire career, she had never given a student an A.

Everyone called her Killer Keller. Even other teachers.

Patricia Lee Gauch, Editor

G. P. PUTNAM'S SONS
Published by the Penguin Group
Penguin Group (USA) LLC
375 Hudson Street, New York NY 10014

USA | Canada | UK | Ireland | Australia
New Zealand | India | South Africa | China
penguin.com
A Penguin Random House Company

Library of Congress
Cataloging-in-Publication Data
Polacco, Patricia, author, illustrator.
An A from Miss Keller / Patricia Polacco.
pages cm   Summary: Trisha wants to write
something that will please her demanding
writing teacher, who is rumored to have never
given a student an A.   [1. Teacher-student
relationships—Fiction. 2. Authorship—
Fiction.] I. Title.   PZ7.P75186Aam 2015
[E]—dc23   2014042039

Manufactured in China by RR Donnelley Asia
Printing Solutions Ltd.
ISBN 978-0-399-16691-4
10 9 8 7 6 5 4 3 2 1

Design by Siobhán Gallagher.
Text set in 13-point Garth Graphic Std.
The illustrations are rendered in pencils
and markers.

An Ⓐ from Miss Keller

Patricia Polacco

G. P. Putnam's Sons
An Imprint of Penguin Group (USA)

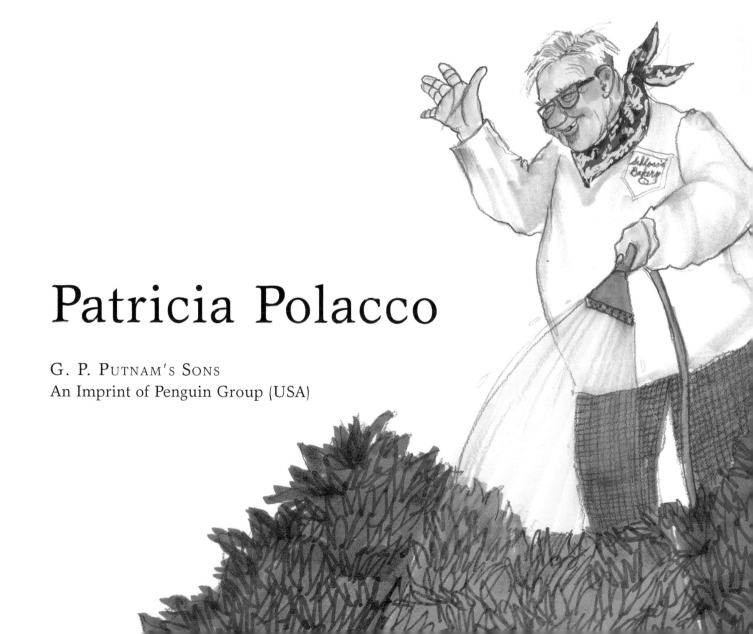

On the first day of class, Miss Keller slithered into the room, and strutting up and down the aisles, snarled, "I am going to transform each and every one of you into a crackerjack writer! One enormous miracle, right?

"But," she barked in a deep Southern accent, "if you think this class is going to be simple, head for the door right now. You are going to work harder than you have ever worked in your entire miserable little lives. Some of you may not make it through the term!"

I felt as if she was looking right at me.

Miss Keller seemed taller than she really was. She stood stiff and erect, but when she was at her desk, she reminded me of a bird of prey perched on a dead limb, ready to swoop down on one of us.

"Your first assignment is going to be an essay. I expect you to dazzle me. Impress me. Send me into ecstasy with your brilliance.

"I want to see if you deserve to be here at all! The subject? Your families and your home life—the inside story." We all scrambled, took out paper, and started to write.

"No, no! Not in class!" she boomed. We all dropped our pencils. "This is a homework assignment. Three full pages and no grammatical errors. Due tomorrow!"

I swallowed hard.

The whole way home, all I could think about was that essay. It just had to be good!

I turned up the hill and walked toward my house. Pop Schloss, our next-door neighbor, was sitting on his front steps. He lived alone, wife gone, kids grown. He patted the step next to him.

"Bad day?" he asked, pulling a bag from his pocket and offering me a newly baked cookie. Pop, known far and wide for being a master pastry chef, always carried cookies in his pocket.

"I have the meanest teacher in the whole school!"

"Not Killer Keller?" Pop pretended to hold his head in shock. I nodded. "Hmmm. Both of my sons had her in school. Remind me to tell you a story about her sometime."

We both just sat and watched the birds land on the telephone wire across the street. Like I said, that essay had to be good.

That night, I took to my desk and began to write. I loved my room, and it was a big part of my home life, so I looked around and began to describe it. In detail! I wrote about how I loved my cat, my mom, my new skirt, eating breakfast—I felt masterful. This was, I thought, some of the best writing I had ever done.

I could hardly wait to read it out loud in class.

The next morning, one by one, my classmates read their essays out loud. I wasn't afraid to read, but I was sure nervous. Then I heard my name.

"Miss Barber, you're next."

I read my masterpiece about my family, my home life, about how I loved everyone and everything about it. I was sure Miss Keller would be impressed, but she started pacing.

"Miss Barber, you used the word *love* to describe your cat, your skirt, your neighbor, a pile of pancakes . . . and your mother. Do you feel the same about a plate of pancakes as you do your mother? Words convey feelings. But there are differences!

"Class, take out a piece of paper and make a list of words that convey love. But . . . *love* is the one word you cannot use."

We all tried, but our lists were very, very short.

"All right, class." She swept to the front of the room. "Do you know what a thesaurus is? And no, it is not a prehistoric lizard!" No one could answer. "That is your assignment for tonight. Figure it out, bring a thesaurus to class, and look up the word *love*."

After I got home that afternoon, I ran next door to see Pop.

"A thesaurus? I think I still have mine that the boys used when they had Miss Keller," he bubbled as he trundled into their old room.

"And yes siree, here it is!" He pulled out a small paperback from a pile of books. "All the words are listed in alphabetical order. And in the back? Word choices—over 150,000. If I remember Miss Keller, this book will be your bible from now on."

That very next day, Miss Keller wrote a list of words on the board—*content*, *cool*, *loyal*—and told us to use our thesaurus to list as many alternatives to each word as we could find. Whoever got the longest lists would be excused from the Friday quiz.

Guess what? I had the longest lists! I had actually done something right! No quiz. But out at recess Eric Yangden and Tim Farkus started teasing, "Looks like the dumbbell is teacher's new pet!"

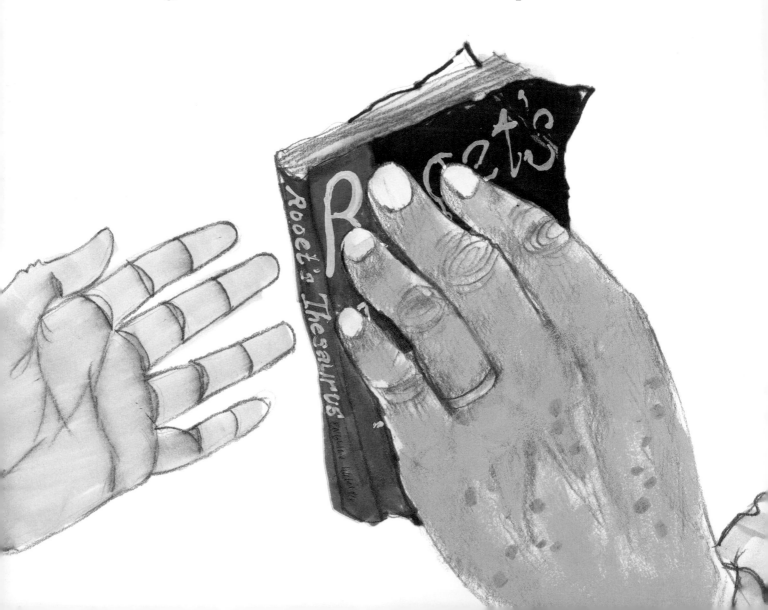

As the days passed, Miss Keller gave our class all kinds of writing exercises to do. Sometimes in the classroom, sometimes out. We went outside one day to listen to trees—to sharpen our senses, Miss Keller said. We listened in on conversations in the lunchroom for a dialogue assignment. To begin to understand color, we went to the town dump!

One day, she brought a bunch of objects right into the classroom—handlebars, a screwdriver, a cup—set them out, and told us, "Look at each object and make a list of what we could use them for, except for the use they were meant for."

For homework that night, she asked us to interview an older person about an object in his or her house that meant something to him or her—a pretty dish or tablecloth, a figurine. She called it a "found object."

Of course I knew exactly whom I was going to interview.

Pop!

Pop and I walked around his house together. "What are you going to pick as your 'found object,' Pop?" I asked. He just couldn't seem to decide. After a time, he walked over to his mantel and took down a beautiful photograph.

"This lovely woman is my Millie. I was in love with her from the first moment I laid eyes on her," he whispered quietly. "She was so lovely, Patricia. When she walked into a room, the sun and moon would peek into the window just to get a glimpse of her. Oh, how I miss her," his voice trailed off.

He talked to me about his Millie for the next hour. I started writing before I left his house.

I was sure I nailed it this time. I wrote with oodles of heart and feeling. I couldn't wait for Miss Keller to see this essay. But when she handed it back, there was a C scrawled at the bottom. Again.

What did she want from me anyway? She kept me after school that day.

"Miss Barber, your paper on your neighbor's Millie was, well, adequate. But where are the words that truly show emotion?" Then she turned and looked right at me. "The reader needs to FEEL what you feel, Miss Barber, but not in an ordinary way. Be daring, unexpected, surprising . . . original!"

Now she gazed deeply into my eyes. "You have the words, Patricia. You have to give them wings!"

That day I found Pop out in his backyard feeding his koi fish in the pond. Pop could see I was upset.

I told him everything. That the boys in class were still calling me "teacher's pet" even though Miss Keller was harder on me than anyone. That today she'd said I lacked emotional connection in my writing.

"My guess is old Killer Keller has taken a real interest in you, or she would have just let you sit there like a bump on a log. As for the teasing, do you know what my first name is? It's Lynn. The guys in my class loved that, and I was the only boy in the cooking class, too. They never let me live that down, either!"

The two of us laughed so hard, we could hardly catch our breath. I had noticed before that Pop sometimes took pills. He said they were "to keep his ticker going." I knew that meant his heart. Today I noticed he slipped two pills under his tongue.

Days with Miss Keller seemed to fly by—none of them easy for me.

Then one day, she called us together. "Today, I am assigning you the dreaded term essay!" I'd heard about it, all right! "I have taught you many forms of writing: dialogue and scene, opinion essay, personal narrative . . . choose one of these for this last big assignment, and choose well. The grade I give you may well determine if you pass!"

I was already sweating. To make things worse, she asked me to stay after "for a little chat."

"Patricia," she said, "I hope you choose a personal narrative, because quite frankly your writing still lacks emotional connection with the reader."

But no matter how hard I tried, I couldn't come up with a subject for my term essay emotional enough for Miss Keller.

The last Sunday before my deadline to hand in the topic, all of us kids—Stewart, Winnie, Chantille—were at Pop's baking cookies for a block party to help raise money for Mrs. Scudder across the street. She had fallen down her back stairs and broken bones.

As we were rolling the cookies out, Stewart asked me how I liked Miss Keller. I told him that no matter what I did, no matter what I wrote, it didn't seem to please her. "To top it all off," I said, "tomorrow our topic is due for the term essay, and I don't have one!"

"That reminds me! I told you that I'd tell you a story about Miss Keller," Pop said thoughtfully as he rolled out a ball of cookie dough. "All of you kids know she is one tough teacher. But not too long ago she came across one of the most talented writers she'd seen. She picked apart everything he wrote, had him do it over—and over—until he got it right.

"Truth is, he'd never worked so hard for a teacher in his life."

"So what happened to that kid, Pop?" Stewart asked.

"Well, he became a writer. Went to work for the biggest newspaper in Chicago! Then to the biggest paper in Washington, DC. He covered stories from South America to the Middle East to Soviet Russia. Once, he won a Pulitzer Prize for reporting."

"He probably would have gone on to do that anyway, Miss Keller or not."

"Not really, Trisha. This boy's family could never have afforded to send him to college. Miss Keller not only taught him how to write, she raised money for his tuition and fees and personally saw to it that he attended journalism school. Otherwise, he might have ended up working in his father's bakery," Pop said with a glint in his eye.

"That's right. That kid was my very own son . . . and I, for one, am grateful for that dogged high-spirited woman! Killer Keller. Without her, well, who knows . . ."

He slipped another pill under his tongue.

Not a week later—still with no essay topic—I'd come early to Miss Keller's class when the office secretary came in and gave a note to her. "Miss Barber," Miss Keller said. "We need to go to the office." She looked shocked and sad.

When we got to the office, my mother was there. I could see she had been crying. She told me Pop had passed away that morning. A sudden heart attack.

As we pulled into our garage, I saw Pop's sons. They looked so heartbroken. All I wanted was to go through his house one last time. His sons invited me over. I walked through every room. Touched his pillow on his bed. Ran my hand across the back of his favorite chair. Held his bakery coat that he wore when we helped him make cookies. I couldn't stop crying. The sky wasn't happy anymore. How could the earth still be turning when someone like Pop had left it.

That night, I sat at my desk and started writing. I wrote and wrote and wrote.

It seemed like the whole neighborhood was at Pop's funeral. Even Miss Keller. And the shops on College Avenue closed for the day. Everything looked different somehow. My sadness hurt everywhere.

Long after it was due, I placed the piece I had written the day Pop died on Miss Keller's desk. I didn't really care anymore whether I impressed her or not. All that mattered was how I felt about him.

A few days later, I got a pink slip from Miss Keller to come and see her. My heart almost stopped. Anyone who got a pink slip was about to get real bad news because it was the end of the term. She must have hated my essay!

I started sobbing. First Pop, now this. I didn't even know if I would pass.

But when I walked into her room, she actually took both my hands. "Patricia dear, I am so sorry for your loss," she said. Then I saw my essay folded in half on her desk.

"I have graded your essay," she began. "I don't want you to unfold it until you are home, do you understand?" I shook my head yes.

Then she did something that startled me. She hugged me. She actually hugged me!

Then she whispered, "Patricia, you wrote a stunning tribute to Pop. The crowning example of a personal narrative."

My heart sang as I ran all the way home with my essay still folded in my hand.

As I climbed the hill, I stopped and looked up at Pop's house for a moment.

"You're with Millie now, Pop!" I whispered. That thought made me warm inside.

Then I opened my folded paper. There, written in red across the top of the cover sheet: "Patricia, your spelling still leaves much to be desired; however, you've given your words wings! I am departing from my custom . . . here is your A."

My heart warms whenever I think of Miss Keller. She later told me that she was impressed with how I used Pop's very own thesaurus to write my papers. I remember his notes were in the margins in his own handwriting. When I read them, it seemed to bring me closer to him.

Certainly, I did use the word "love." However, I used every form of it. To this day, when I think of Pop and Miss Keller, my thoughts soar, for I shall always regard them as "beloved."

Patricia Polacco